Abridged English Classics

# Around The World in 80 Days

**Jules Verne**

ibs BOOKS (UK)

**Around The World In 80 Days**

Verne, Jules

English Classics Series



First Edition : 2008

Published by
ibs BOOKS (UK)
55, Warren Street,
London W1T 5NW
email: info@ibsbooks.co.uk

Printed in India on woodfree paper

# Index

# About The Author

**Jules Gabriel Verne** (1828-1905) was a French writer. He is known to be the pioneer of science fiction. His best known works include the magnificent classics like *Twenty Thousand Leagues under the Sea (first pub.1870, transl. to English, 1873)* and *Around the World in Eighty Days (1873).*

Jules Verne was born on February 8, 1828, in the sea-port town of Nantes, France. As a boy, Jules liked sitting at the docks and listening to sailors' tales of faraway places. He often dreamt about travelling to unknown destinations and discovering new wonders of the world.

When Jules was twelve years old, he ran off to be a cabin boy on a merchant ship bound for India. Fortunately, he was found and returned to his parents. His father punished the young by with a severe beating.

This made Jules promise, "From now on, I'll travel only in my imagination."

And he did just that! Jules spent many hours studying geology, engineering, and astronomy. All this knowledge he used in his stories and novels. He fulfilled his childhood promise and let his imagination take him and his readers to all sorts of wonderful journeys. He wrote tales of journeying inside volcanoes, under oceans, over unexplored countries and even to the moon and distant planets.

His first novel *Five Weeks in a Balloon* was published in 1863. Soon he started writing novels such as *Journey to the Center of the Earth* (1864) and *From the Earth to the Moon* (1866). The public loved reading about the wonderful journeys that he described in his novels and stories. People felt thrilled to read about the heroes that travelled in balloons, steam tanks, rocket ships, submarines, electric autos and mechanically-driven autos.

Jules thought about all these inventions at the time when people still travelled by horse and carriage, steam engines were just being developed and electricity had just been discovered. It was thirty years after Jules wrote about a submarine in his famous novel

*'20,000 Leagues Under the Sea'* that the first actual submarine was built.

The wonderful tales that Jules Verne told not only made him famous and rich, they also introduced the genre of science fiction in literature.

Jules Verne died in the city of Amines on March 24, 1905. By the time of his death, many of the inventions that he had described in his novels had become reality. His work inspired many scientists to try and create the wonderful things that Jules had described in his novels and stories. Perhaps, that's the reason why the U.S. Navy honoured this great writer by naming its first atomic submarine – the U.S.S. *Nautilus.*

Jules Verne shall forever be remembered not just as a writer who gave the world many glorious tales of discovery and adventure, but also as the man who "Invented the future."

One

# Phileas Fogg and Passepartout

Mr. Phileas Fogg was a truly intriguing English gentleman, who resided at No. 7 Saville Row in London. He spent most of his time at the Reform Club, reading in the library there or playing whist, a popular English card-game. Otherwise, he kept mostly to himself. He did not hold a regular job, yet seemed to be quite well-off, and everyone was clueless where all his money came from.

The most outstanding thing about Phileas Fogg was that he religiously followed the clock. His own clock told not only the hour, minute and second, but also the month and year. He was always precisely on time, and his activities followed the same pattern day after day.

Every morning, at exactly 11:30 , Phileas Fogg went to the Reform Club. He ate a solitary lunch and dinner there everyday at exactly the same time, even so at the same table in the same room. At exactly midnight, he reached back home and went straight off to bed.

Phileas Fogg had no family, close relatives or good friends at all. He had shared his huge house with a single servant, but because of his fanaticism for precision, he had recently fired him for bringing shaving water that was a few degrees too cold. Now he was looking for someone to replace the other servant.

One particular day, there was a knock at the door, and a young man entered.

Phileas Fogg greeted the man and asked him, " Have you come all the way from France for the job of a servant? What is your name?"

The young man replied, "Please call me Jean. My last name is Passepartout."

"Passepartout?"

"Yes, a name I decided upon myself. I have continually been moving from one job to another. I have worked as a singer, a circus performer, a gym teacher and a fireman. Then, five years ago, I left France to become a domestic servant here in England. I had to leave that job too, but now I hope to settle down here with you and forget all about this befitting name- Passepartout."

"Good! What time is it by your watch?"

"11:25."

"Oh, you're four minutes slow," sighed Phileas Fogg. "But never mind! Starting now, at 11:29 on Wednesday, October 2, you are in my service."

Two

# Passepartout Starts Afresh

Passepartout observed Phileas Fogg carefully during their first meeting, and he was quite impressed by him. Mr. Fogg was a tall, handsome man, with light coloured hair and a moustache, pale skin, and aged around 40. Passepartout, on the other hand, had a very good build and his muscles had become very strapping from his days in the circus and the gym.

However, the personalities of the master and the servant were in contrast to each other : the master was quiet and reserved, while the servant was vivacious and talkative.

Would Passepartout be able to adapt to Fogg's systematic and orderly lifestyle? He had not fared too well in other English households, partly because he was very outspoken. His most recent job had ended quickly when he had told his own master off for coming home drunk.

That very day, Mr. Fogg left for the Reform Club, and Passepartout began looking around the house. Everything was neat and tidy, and in order. Mr. Fogg's clothes and shoes even had numbers marked upon them, showing what time of the year they were to be worn. Passepartout came to survey his own room right after. There was a large clock in his room that was to be precisely timed to the second with the one in Phileas Fogg's room. On the wall above the clock was a list of the things Passepartout would have to do. He learned from reading the list that Fogg awoke at exactly 8:00 each morning and left for the Reform Club at exactly 11:30. His duties would include serving his master toast and tea at 8:23, bringing his shaving water at 9:37 and helping him get dressed starting at 9:40. There would be many other chores to attend to between 11:30, when Fogg left the house, and midnight, when he went to bed.

Passepartout began to think of Phileas Fogg as some kind of machine, but he continued to look forward to his new job as a welcome change from the past.

## Three

# The Bet

At exactly 11:30, Phileas Fogg set off for the Reform Club. His regular table was set for- lunch. He finished eating at exactly 14 minutes before 1:00 and went to the library. It took him until 3:45 to read the Times, and until dinner time to finish the *Standard*. He finished dinner at 5:40. Half an hour later, his whist partners arrived: Andrew Stuart, an engineer; two bankers, John Sullivan and Samuel Fallentin; Thomas Flanagan, a beer brewer; and Gautier Ralph, the director of the Bank of England.

A robbery of 55,000 pounds had just occurred at the bank. According to a witness, the robber was dressed like an English gentleman. The witness had described him to the police, and detectives were sent all over England and to the English territories overseas to catch him. A reward of 2,000 pounds had been offered for his capture.

"The robber will surely get away," said Stuart. "The world is certainly big enough to hide him."

"It was, once," said Phileas Fogg, He put down his cards and declared, "Gentlemen, it is now possible to go around the world in 80 days! From London to Suez by railroad and steamboat would take 7 days; from Suez to Bombay, India, by rail, 13 days; from Bombay to Calcutta by rail, 3 days; from Calcutta to Hong Kong by steamer, 13 days; from Hong Kong to Yokohama, Japan, by steamer, 6 days; from Japan -to California by steamer, 22 days; from California to New York by rail, 7 days; and from New York back to London by steamer and rail, 9 days. Altogether, that makes 80 days!"

"That may be so," said Stuart, "but you might have bad weather, a railroad accident, a shipwreck, or an Indian attack."

"Even so, the trip could be made in 80 days. Shall we try it, Mr. Stuart?"

"No, not me! But I'll bet 4,000 pounds that it can't be done."

"I have 20,000 pounds in the bank, and I'll bet it all!" Fogg declared. "I can leave tonight. I'll take the train for Dover at 8:45. Today is Wednesday, October 2, I'll be back in this very room on Saturday, December 21, at 8:45. Otherwise, all my money is yours!"

Phileas Fogg wrote out a check for 20,000 pounds. This was half his fortune. He would need the other half for travel expenses.

It was 7:00 by then, and Fogg's whist partners offered to put the cards away so Mr. Fogg could get ready for his trip.

"I'm ready right now," Fogg replied. "Please deal the cards, gentlemen!"

Four

# The Departure

Phileas Fogg left the Reform Club at 7.25, much earlier than his normal routine. Passepartout was amazed when his master arrived home long before his usual return at midnight. Fogg hurriedly said, "We're leaving for Dover, England in ten minutes!"

"Are you leaving home, sir?"

"Yes. We're going around the world. We have to be back within 80 days! There's no time to waste at all!"

Passepartout was astounded. Finally, he asked, "What about the suitcases?"

"There's no time to fetch the suitcases. Just pack a bag with two shirts and three pairs of socks for each of us. Bring my coat, raincoat, and some walking shoes too, and hurry!"

The servant was stunned, and for a moment he thought it was a joke. However, he did as he was told- he packed a bag, to which Fogg added a railroad and steamboat timetable and a large roll of banknotes.

"Be careful with this bag," Fogg warned. "There is 20,000 pounds in cash inside!"

Phileas Fogg and Passepartout called a taxi and reached the railroad station at 8:20. A beggar holding a baby in her arms approached them. Fogg took out all the money he had just won at whist, and gave it to her. Turning away, he raced to the ticket counter. He then bought first-class tickets for France for himself and his aide. The train pulled out at. exactly 8:45.

❐❐❐

Five

# Rumour Has It

Phileas Fogg's bet became famous all over the country and it made its way to all the newspapers. The people gambled on Fogg's chances to make the trip in 80 days. Some thought it could indeed be done, but most believed Fogg was foolish and had been defrauded by his 'friends' at the Reform Club.

'Phileas Fogg bonds' were sold everywhere. However, their value fell drastically with the rumour that Fogg was the gentleman who had robbed the Bank of England.

A certain Detective Fix had discovered Fogg's true identity. The chief of the London police sent him to Suez, Egypt, to look for the robber. He also promised to send an arrest warrant after him.

Egypt was then a part of the British Empire, and the Suez Canal had been built as a shortcut for the ships travelling between England and India, which was also an important British territory.

Upon hearing the rumors about Phileas Fogg being the robber, the people suddenly recalled his odd habits and his reserved nature. They viewed his around-the-world trip as a pretext for him to leave London before the police could arrest him. Why else would he lay a large sum like 20,000 pounds on the line?

Six

# The Arrival at Suez

At 11:00 A.M. on October 9, the English steamer *Mongolia was* due in Suez. Detective Fix waited worriedly on the deck.

"How will you identify the robber even if he's on the ship?" asked the English consul. "From the way the London police described him, he looks like an honest man."

"Don't worry, consul. I've arrested plenty of robbers. I'll know this one if I see him. He won't get away!"

"I hope you're right, Mr. Fix!"

"The robber would be foolish to travel on to India, wouldn't he?" Fix asked.

"Maybe not," replied the consul. "If he's smart, he'll go to India because he knows the police wouldn't expect him to!"

The *Mongolia* arrived right on time. One of the passengers approached Fix to ask where the consul's office was. His passport had to be stamped with a visa to show that he had stopped at Suez.

Fix flipped through the passport. The picture of the passport-holder caught the attention of the detective. It matched the description of the London bank robber.

"Is this your passport?" the detective asked.

"No, it belongs to my master."

"He must appear before the consul *in person* in order to get a visa," said Fix firmly.

Seven

# Suez And Off Again

"I think I've got my man!" shouted Fix, bursting into the consul's office.

. "That may be so, Mr. Fix, but I don't think he'll give away his identity that easily and come to see me. A robber just doesn't let people know where he is. Besides, the passport doesn't really need to be stamped with a visa at Suez."

"If he comes, don't give him a visa," begged Fix, hoping to keep the robber in Suez until the arrest warrant arrived.

"I can't refuse the visa," said the consul. "Arresting him is your problem, not mine."

A knock sounded, and a man entered the room to request a visa.

"Are you Phileas Fogg?" asked the consul, eyeing the passport.

"Yes, sir."

"And who is this man?"

"My servant, Passepartout."

"Where are you going?"

"To Bombay, India."

"You don't need a visa."

"I know that, but I want to prove that I passed through Suez."

The consul stamped the passport, unaware that Fogg needed the visa to prove to his friends that he had won his bet honestly.

Phileas Fogg returned to the steamer and took out his diary. He noted his arrival in Suez -after traveling through England, France and Italy. Six and one-half of Fogg's 80 days were used up. He was exactly on schedule.

Not bothering to see the incredible sights of Suez, Fogg closed his date book and sat down to breakfast. He was always much more anxious about time, anyway.

Eight

# Fix Confronts Passepartout

Detective Fix joined Passepartout outside the consulate and initiated a conversation.

"Well, how do you like Suez?"

"We are traveling so fast that I can hardly remember where we are."

"This is Suez, a city in Egypt."

"That means we are on the continent of Africa!" said Passepartout. "I never thought that my master and I would travel further than Paris. I would have loved to stay in Paris, but we just whizzed through."

"You must be in a great hurry."

"I'm not, but my master is. We didn't even pack suitcases - only a carpet bag. I have to buy some clothes here." "

Fix was taken aback and excited by these remarks. He assured the servant that there was plenty of time to go to a men's store.

"It's only 12:00," said Passepartout.

"Your watch is slow," said Fix.

"That's impossible!"

"Then it must be set for London time, which is two hours behind that of Suez. You should reset your watch when you travel to other countries."

"Reset my watch? Never!"

"It won't agree with the sun if you don't reset it."

"Too bad for the sun," declared the servant, putting the watch in his pocket.

"Did you leave London in a hurry?" asked Fix.

"You bet we did! Last Friday night at 8:00, my master came home from his club, and less than an hour later we were gone."

"But where is your master going?"

"Around the world in 80 days! He says he made a bet that he could do it, but that's too crazy to believe. Something else must be afoot."

"Ah! So is Mr. Fogg a strange man?"

"Extremely strange."

"Is he wealthy?"

"He must be. He's carrying loads of brand new banknotes with him, and he offered the captain of the *Mongolia* a reward if he gets us to India ahead of schedule. By the way, is Bombay far from here?"

"Yes," answered Fix, "it's a ten-day trip by sea."

"Oh dear," sighed Passepartout; "my gas burner will be on for a long time. My gas bill will be higher than the wages my master pays me."

' Fix wasn't listening any more. He had already made a dash for the consul's office.

"I've found the robber for sure," he shouted, as he burst into the room. "He pretends to be traveling around the world on a bet with some friends. He laid a wager that he could make the journey in 80 days."

"`He's a smart fellow," said the consul. "He'll throw the police off his track and then return to London."

"Very smart, indeed" -

Fix decided to follow Fogg to Bombay. He sent a telegraph to London asking the police to send the arrest warrant to India. Then he boarded the steamer *Mongolia* headed for Bombay.

❒❒❒

Nine

# Onto India

The steamer sped across the Red Sea and the Indian Ocean. Phileas Fogg entertained himself by playing whist, and with four wholesome meals each day. Passepartout, on the other hand, went up to the deck.

"What a pleasant surprise to see you again!" said the servant, catching sight of Detective Fix. "Where are you traveling to?"

"To Bombay. I work for an English company there," answered Fix, taking care not to divulge the true nature of his mission.

"Well, I hope to see the sights in India," said Passepartout. "I find it rather stupid bustling from one ship to the train, onto the next ship, and so on, leave alone this whole issue of going around the world in eighty days"

"Maybe your master is going to perform some secret assignment during this trip," said Fix, hoping to get some more information about Fogg's plans.

"If so, I am clueless," Passepartout replied.

The *Mongolia* stopped at Aden, in Arabia, to restore the supply of coal, and on October 20 (two days ahead of schedule), it sailed into Bombay. Phileas Fogg gave the captain a large reward for giving him those two extra days. He felt they would be well needed later in the journey.

Ten

# The Servant and His Shoes

Phileas Fogg and Passepartout left the steamer at 4:00. In four hours the train would depart from Bombay, on the west coast of India, for Calcutta, in the northeast.

Not bothering about the truly incredible sights of India, Fogg went directly to the consulate for a visa and then to the railroad station to dine.

Detective Fix, still on the trail, however, went to the police station, but the arrest warrant for the bank robber had not yet arrived.

Passepartout, on the other hand, went off to purchase shirts and socks for his master. Later, he ambled into a beautiful Indian temple.

It is customary to remove your shoes before you enter a temple, and Passepartout, unaware of this, walked in with his shoes on. No sooner had he entered the building than three Indian priests knocked him down, tore off his shoes, and beat him with their fists. Passepartout leaped to his feet, knocked over two of his attackers, and fled to escape the third.

At five minutes before 8:00, the servant, shoeless, dashed into the railroad station and told Phileas Fogg what had happened. Fix, hiding nearby, overheard the conversation.

"Oh, the servant has commited a crime in India. That gives me an opportunity to arrest the master. After all, Fogg must be held responsible for his servant's actions."

Eleven

# The Forest Delay

As the train departed from the station, Phileas Fogg caught sight of a certain Sir Francis Cromarty, one of his whist partners from the steamer. Sir Francis, an English army officer, spent most of his time in India and knew the country as well as any Indian. Fogg, however, wasn't interested in learning more about India. He was too busy figuring out how many days and hours of his around-the-world trip had gone past.

"See those mountains?" said Sir Francis. "A few years ago, the train would be delayed to such an extent here that you would have lost all hope of winning your bet. The railroad would terminate here, and then the passengers would have to cross the mountains on horseback."

"That wouldn't have wrecked my travel plans at all," said Phileas Fogg, impulsively. "I was quite certain there would be problems along the way."

"Indeed, but you may just run into trouble over your servant's ignorant behavior at the temple. The government safeguards the Indian religions and the customs very strictly."

At 8:00, the train halted, right in the middle of a forest. The conductor commanded all the passengers to get off.

"Where are we?" asked Phileas Fogg.

"At the village of Kholby," replied the conductor. "The railroad terminates here. There is no railroad from here to Allahabad, a distance of 50 miles."

"But the newspapers said that the railroad runs throughout India now," Fogg protested.

"The papers made a mistake"

"Why, then, do you sell tickets from Bombay to Calcutta?"

"With the understanding that passengers will find their own way of getting from Kholby to Allahabad."

"This is a terrible delay for you,. Mr. Fogg," said Sir Francis.

"It's okay. I'm two days ahead of schedule. Today is October 22. A steamer leaves Calcutta for Hong Kong on October 25. We will reach Calcutta by that time."

Fogg spotted a man with an elephant and

decided to buy the animal at any cost to make it to Calcutta. The owner didn't want to sell the animal but finally accepted 2,000 pounds for it. Fogg then hired a young Parsee man of India to serve as their guide and elephant driver. Phileas Fogg and Sir Francis sat on the elephant's neck, whereas Passepartout sat on its back, and they finally set off for Calcutta.

Twelve

# To The Rescue

The travelers passed through an area peopled by fierce tribes, renowned for their savage customs. Suddenly, the elephant stopped. Loud voices could be heard through the trees.

"A procession of Brahmins is heading this way," said the Parsee. "Let's hide!"

"Who are the Brahmins?"

"They are the priests of the religion of Hinduism"

Soon the priests came into view, followed by a large chanting crowd. Carried along on a platform was a statue of the Hindu goddess Kali, four-armed and red-bodied. The Brahmins also dragged along a bejeweled young woman dressed in a beautiful robe. She had very light skin and looked more like a European than an Indian. Behind her came men wielding sabers and guns, and carrying the body of an old man dressed like a Hindu prince. The Parsee explained that the body was that of the young woman's husband, who was an Indian prince.

"The woman will be taken to a temple to spend the night," said the Parsee. "Tomorrow at dawn, she will be burned alive as a human sacrifice to the gods"

Phileas Fogg, aghast, cried out in shock.

"Let us save her"

"But, sir.."

"I have 12 hours to spare. Let us help the poor woman"

❏❏❏

Thirteen

# Saving Aouda

Aouda, as the young woman was called, was famous for her beauty. She was yet another Parsee. The daughter of a rich merchant of Bombay, Aouda had received an English education. After her father passed away, she was forced to marry the old rajah. Miserable with her new life, she had run away. However, she was caught and brought back. Now, she faced a horrible death.

The would-be rescuers hid in the trees near the temple, awaiting nightfall. They hoped to slip past the Brahmins into the temple, but guards with torches and sabers watched all the entrances. Passepartout, noticing that the Brahmins were drunk, began to work on another plan of rescue.

Dawn came, and the hour of sacrifice was at hand. The Brahmins built a funeral pyre, and laid the rajah's body on it. Then the priests led Aouda out of the temple. She had, visibly, been drugged and was unable to free herself. She was placed beside her husband's corpse.

The priests poured oil all over the funeral pyre and set a torch to it. Flames leaped up at once.

Suddenly, cries of terror came from the crowd. The old rajah was alive!

He stood up, took his wife in his arms, and, surrounded by fire and smoke, climbed down from the funeral pyre.

He walked over to the hidden Phileas Fogg, and signaled that they should leave at once.

Passepartout was disguised as the "rajah." In the moments before dawn, under the cover of darkness, he had hidden the body of the real rajah and had allowed himself to be laid on the funeral pyre instead.

Aouda, still in a drugged sleep, was lifted onto the elephant, and the travelers rode quickly through the forest. The Brahmins soon discovered the ploy, and began chasing the elephant, shooting bullets and arrows. It was too late for them, however. Aouda was already a safe distance away.

❒❒❒

Fourteen

# Onto Calcutta

Passepartout was overjoyed at the success of his rescue mission. Sir Francis, however, cautioned that if Aouda didn't leave India she would be recaptured soon, and later, sacrificed.

At 10:00, the travelers arrived at the Allahabad railroad station.

Phileas Fogg bade farewell to the Parsee, not only paying him the money promised for his services, but leaving the elephant to him as well. Fogg, Passepartout, Aouda and Sir Francis then boarded the. train for Calcutta.

As the effect of the drugs wore off, Aouda slowly awoke. She was undoubtedly stunning, and even conversed fluently in English. She found herself dressed in European clothes and traveling on a train with perfect strangers. Fogg offered to take her away from India so that she could prevent recapture. He invited her to travel with him to the British colony of Hong Kong, which lay off the coast of China.

Aouda, in turn, told him of her cousin, Jeejeeh, who lived in Hong Kong itself and could assist her.

Sir Francis got off the train at Benares. The next morning, the train arrived at Calcutta. Phileas Fogg had gained two days between London and Bombay and lost two days traveling across India. So, all in all, he was exactly on schedule.

Fifteen

# The Trial

"Are you Mr. Phileas Fogg?" enquired a policeman at the Calcutta station.

"Yes, I am"

"And is this man your servant?"

"Yes, he is."

"Please follow me."

Fogg. Passepartout and Aouda were led to a room with barred windows.

"You must appear before the judge at 8:30," said the policeman.

"We have been imprisoned!" screamed Passepartout. "Now we shall not make it to the Hong Kong steamer on time."

"Leave me here and go," said Aouda. "If you hadn't rescued me, you would not have been imprisoned here."

"Don't be silly," snapped Phileas Fogg. "Besides, we'll all be on the steamer by noon."

At 8:30, the policeman led the prisoners to a courtroom. Three priests stood before the judge. They had charged Fogg and Passepartout with misbehavior in a holy place.

"I admit we are at fault," cried out Fogg, "but else, they would have sacrificed this poor female at the pyre!"

"That's right," added Passepartout. "These priests are from the temple of Pillaji."

"No," said the priests. "We are from Bombay. Here is the pair of shoes that was left behind."

"Those are mine!" cried Passepartout.

Detective Fix had, in fact, promised the priests a reward if they would follow Passepartout to Calcutta. Fix was, even now, hidden in the courtroom.

His plan was to delay Phileas Fogg so that he could not leave India before the arrest warrant arrived from London.

"Since you have admitted your guilt," the judge told Passepartout, "and since English law protects Indian religions very strictly, I order you to spend 15 days in jail and pay a fine of 300 pounds."

The judge then turned to Phileas Fogg.

"The master must be responsible for the actions of his servant. Therefore, Mr. Fogg, I command you to spend a week in jail and pay a fine of150 pounds."

Fix, gleeful, remained hidden there. A week would surely be enough time for the arrest warrant to arrive.

"I will offer bail," proclaimed Phileas Fogg.

"All right," said the judge, "but the bail will be 1,000 pounds for each man. And if you leave India before your sentence is over, the money will not be returned."

Fix was fuming. The robber would escape once again. He knew Fogg would gladly leave the bail money behind rather than miss the steamer to Hong Kong.

Fogg, Passepartout and Aouda reached the harbor at 11:00, with an hour to spare.

Fix, furious, decided to follow them to Hong Kong.

Sixteen

# Fix Questions Passepartout

Phileas Fogg sailed from India to Hong Kong on the steamer *Rangoon.* During the journey, spanning 10 to 12 days, Aouda began relating the story of her life, and Passepartout, in turn, told her about his master's incredible 20,000 pound bet.

Fogg himself spent long hours in Aouda's company, but rarely spoke to her. He seemed indifferent to her enchanting beauty. Phileas Fogg was very strange indeed!

Fix, however, remained hidden in his cabin for most of the journey. He had asked the London police to send the arrest warrant for the bank robber onto Hong Kong, which was the last British colony Fogg would set foot on during the trip. After Hong-Kong, Fogg would make his way to China, Japan and America. Once he left English soil, the robber might just escape for good.

Did Fix dare tell Passepartout who he really was? He felt sure that the servant had no hand in the bank robbery and didn't have any idea that his master was a bank robber. If Fix could convince Passepartout that he might have to share the responsibility for his master's crime, he could perhaps win over his cooperation in getting Fogg arrested. On the other hand, Passepartout may disclose Fix's real identity.

Fix approached the servant on deck and, with an air of fake surprise, asked what he was doing on the *Rangoon.*

"I should ask you the same question," said Passepartout. "I thought we had left you at Bombay. Are you going around the world too?"

"No," replied the detective. "I will remain in Hong Kong for quite a while. Tell me, how is Mr. Fogg?"

"He's quite well and still on schedule. Did you know that we also have a young lady traveling with us?"

Fix again faked surprise. Passepartout told him about their ventures in India, including the rescue of Aouda and the issue with the shoes in the temple at Bombay. He didn't know, of course, that Fix had plotted to put him in trouble with the Bombay priests.

"Are you taking the young lady to Europe?" the detective asked.

"No. We will leave her with a cousin of hers in Hong Kong."

Fix, cautious as ever, saved his other queries for later, fearing that Passepartout would get suspicious.

❑❑❑

Seventeen

## From Singapore to Hongkong

Passepartout did wonder why Fix kept following them around the world, but he could never have guessed Fix's real motive. He concluded that Fix must be a spy sent by the members of the Reform Club to ensure that Phileas Fogg was actually going around the world.

"Gentlemen of the Reform Club," Passepartout said to himself, "you'll be sorry for treating my master like this!"

The servant, however, said nothing to Mr. Fogg, fearing it may insult him.

On October 31, the *Rangoon* sailed into Singapore to take on coal. Phileas Fogg noted in his diary that the ship was a half day ahead of schedule. Hong Kong was still 1,300 miles away. If he could reach Hong Kong in six days, he would be able to catch the steamer for Yokohama, Japan, on November 6.

After Phileas Fogg had left the ship with

Aouda for a carriage ride through Singapore, Fix cornered Passepartout once again.

"You seem to be in a great hurry to reach Hong Kong," he said.

"Yes, indeed," answered Passepartout.

"Mr. Fogg, I presume, wants to catch the steamer for Yokohama?"

"That's right."

"Do you really believe, then, that he intends to go around the world?"

"Of course I do. Don't you?"

"No, I don't believe it."

"You're very cunning," said Passepartout unexpectedly, "Will you follow us all around the world?"

"I'm not sure. " Fix answered nervously.

"Ah, but you should definfitely come with us. You have already pursued us from Suez to India and now to China. We're going to Japan next, and then onto America!"

Fix was getting more and more panicky.

"Do you make much money at your job?" asked Passepartout.

"That depends," Fix said. "Sometimes I am lucky. At other times, I am not. However, I don't pay my own travel expenses."

"I'm certain of that," the servant retorted, still holding the impression that the Reform

Club members had hired Fix as a spy.

This conversation ended when Phileas Fogg and Aouda returned to the ship. But Fix was troubled. Had Passepartout guessed who he really was? And, if so, did Phileas Fogg know about him as well?

Eighteen

# Hong Kong

On November 3, a dreadful windstorm struck the steamer. The next day, the sea was calm, but due to the storm, the ship would be delayed by a day: it would arrive on November 6 instead of November 5.

"When can we catch the next ship to Yokohama?" Fogg asked the captain.

"The *Carnatic* leaves tomorrow at high tide. It was supposed to sail yesterday, but one of its boilers had broken down."

Phileas Fogg had indeed been lucky! If the Carnatic's boiler hadn't broken down, she would have sailed, and Fogg would have to wait a week for the next steamer.

Mr Fogg was 24 hours behind schedule, but the time could probably be made up later.

With 16 hours to spare in Hong Kong, Fogg left Passepartout with Aouda and set out to search for the young woman's cousin, Jeejeeh. He learned, however, that the cousin had moved from Hong Kong to Europe. They, thus, had no choice but to take Aouda along on their journey around the world. The young woman was, in fact, delighted by this turn of events. She had secretly fallen in love with Phileas Fogg.

Nineteen

# Passepartout is Drugged

"Have you decided to travel with us to America, Mr. Fix?" asked Passepartout.

"Yes," replied the detective. He was, in fact, determined to stop Phileas Fogg from leaving Hong Kong before the arrest warrant arrived.

"Good!", said the servant, chuckling. "Let's get cabins aboard the Carnatic."

The man at the ticket office announced that the boiler had been fixed and that the Carnatic would sail that very evening. Passepartout wanted to tell Phileas Fogg the good news immediately, but Fix invited him to a tavern.

The customers at the tavern were either drinking liquor or smoking opium, a very powerful sleep-inducing drug. Smokers overcome by the opium were carried to a large bed at one end of the tavern. Passepartout shared a bottle of wine with Fix and then rose to return to Phileas Fogg.

"Wait!" cried Fix. "I must tell you something very important before you leave."

"Tell me tomorrow!" snapped Passepartout. "There is no time now!"

"What I have to say concerns Mr. Fogg."

Passepartout, intrigued, sat down again.

"You have already guessed who I am, haven't you?" began Fix.

"Certainly."

"Then I should tell you everything."

"I already know everything. But let me tell you that those gentlemen have gone to a lot of difficulty and expense for nothing!"

"For nothing?" exclaimed Fix. "This concerns a very large amount of money!"

"Yes, 20,000 pounds."

"It's 55,000 pounds," Fix corrected.

"What?" shouted Passepartout. "Has Mr. Fogg really dared to chance 55,000 pounds? If so, that is all the more reason to hasten and let him know the change in the Carnatic's timetable."

"Stop!" cried Fix. "Help me! If I succeed, I will get 2,000 pounds as a reward and I will hand 500 pounds over to you!"

"Help you?"

"Yes. I must keep Phileas Fogg in Hong

Kong for a few more days."

"Do you know what you're asking for, Mr. Fix? Is it not enough that you pursued my master till here and then even questioned his honesty? These gentlemen you work for also desire to altogether stop him from making his trip around the world. What a shameless plan! And to think you call yourselves gentlemanly! You should return and tell the members of the Reform Club that Phileas Fogg is a sincere man, and he will win his bet fairly!"

"Who do you think I am?" questioned Fix, who was really perplexed by these remarks.

"Mr. Fix, I have already discovered that you have been hired by the members of the Reform Club to try and prevent Phileas Fogg from completing his journey around the world. However, I refrained from telling my master as I didn't want to upset him."

"Mr. Passepartout, I am not a spy for the Reform Club. I am a police detective. Here is my badge to prove it!"

"But what do you want from me?"

"Let me tell you. Mr. Fogg's infamous bet - to travel around the world within simply 80 days- was just a ploy to keep everyone from discovering why he really had to leave London, and that too, in great haste ."

"And why was that?"

"On September 28, a man robbed the Bank Of England. We have identified your master to be the robber. Now, I will need your help to have him arrested. I will received my promised reward of 2,000 pounds right after, and you will get your 500 pounds. So, will you promise to help me?"

"Never!" screamed Passepartout, who was quite drunk by now. "Besides, my master is not a robber!"

"Are you refusing to help me?"

"Yes, I refuse."

"Very well. Let's just forget the entire thing and drink some more," said Fix.

The liquor made Passepartout drowsy. As he leaned weakly against his chair, Fix slipped an opium pipe between his lips. The servant sank into a drugged sleep.

"Good!" Fix chuckled to himself. "Now Mr. Fogg will not come to know of the Carnatic's departure tonight!"

## Twenty

# Onward to Yokohama

Phileas Fogg and Aouda shopped and dined in Hong Kong. When Passepartout failed to appear at bedtime, Fogg decided that he must be enjoying himself before sailing the following morning. Fogg and Aouda reached the harbor to find that the Carnatic had left the night before. There was still no sign of Passepartout

"I'd like to meet your servant. Is he with you?" asked a man on the dock.

It was Detective Fix. He faked surprise at the news of Passepartout's absence.

"Maybe he boarded the *Carnatic* without us," suggested Phileas Fogg.

"Oh, did you plan to sail on the *Carnatic?* So did I. Now we will have to wait a week for the next steamer to Yokohama."

"I'm sure we'll be able to find another boat ready to sail." said Fogg.

That very moment, a sailor approached

them.

"I have a vessel ready for you, sir."

"Does she travel fast?" asked Fogg.

"Certainly. Where do you wish to go?"

"To Yokohama."

"No! I can't possibly take you that far!"

"I missed the steamer *Carnatic,*" Fogg explained: "I must reach Yokohama by November 14 in order to catch a boat for America. I can offer you 100 pounds per day, plus 200 pounds extra as a reward for getting me there on time."

"I'm really apologetic, sir," said the captain. "It's too dangerous to make such a long journey in my tiny boat, especially at this time of year. Anyway, Yokohama, is more than 1,600 miles from Hong Kong. We'd never make it on time. Maybe something else could be arranged."

"What's that?" asked Fogg keenly.

"We could sail to Shanghai, which is only 800 miles from here. The American steamer starts at Shanghai and stops over at Yokohama. The steamer leaves Shanghai on November 11 at 7:00 in the morning. That gives us four days to reach Shanghai."

"It's a deal. My name is Phileas Fogg."

"I am Job Gunsby, captain of the Tankadere."

"Would you like to join us, Mr. Fix?" Fogg asked the detective.

"Yes, and thank you!"

Twenty One

# The Storm And After

Fix was uncomfortable traveling at Phileas Fogg's expense, but he nevertheless felt that the "robber" owed him something for putting him to so much trouble.

"What a smart man Fogg is!" thought Fix. "He'll go all the way to America to throw the police off his track and then settle down to enjoy his stolen wealth!"

By daybreak on November 8, the *Tankadere* had traveled more than 100 miles, and by evening, she had gone 220 miles.

Captain Bunsby, keen on being rewarded, tried his best to reach Shanghai on time. The following day, however, a terrible storm hit the ship.

"It's a typhoon!" shouted the captain. "We must sail for the nearest port!!"

"We must make it to Shangai at any cost," said Phileas Fogg firmly.

It was futile arguing with him after that.

At 7:00, the hour that the Yokohama steamer was due to depart from Shanghai, Phileas Fogg was three miles from Shanghai harbor. Suddenly the steamer appeared on the waves.

"Signal to her!" Fogg ordered Captain Bunsby: "Hoist your flag!"

Bunsby ran the flag, up at half mast to signal that his ship was in danger. He also fired the small cannon on the deck used in dense fog. They all waited there, hoping the steamer would respond.

❏❏❏

Twenty Two

# Passepartout's side of the story

On November 7 at 6:30 P.M., the Carnatic set sail from Hong Kong with Passepartout on board. He had been carried by two waiters to the bed in the tavern. Struggling against the effects of the opium, he dreamed of his duty to tell Phileas Fogg about the Carnatic's new timetable. Somehow he dragged himself to the harbor and jumped upon the Carnatic just as it was ready to depart. Then he fell into a drugged sleep on the deck.

When Passepartout awoke, the ship was already 150 miles from Hong Kong. The servant recalled with horror the events in the tavern.

"At least I didn't miss the steamer," he said to himself. "But I must find Mr. Fogg right away and explain everything!"

Fogg and Aouda were nowhere to be found.

"Can you tell me what cabin Mr. Phileas

Fogg is in?" he asked a crew member.

"Here is the passenger list. Look for yourself!"

Suddenly, Passepartout realized that he hadn't told Fogg that the ship was leaving in the evening itself. Mr. Fogg would surely lose his bet, and there was even the dreadful possibility that he was jailed in Hong Kong!

Twenty Three

# Yokohama City

On November 13, the Carnatic arrived in Yokohama. Passepartout was all by himself in a strange land and had no money at all. By the following day, he was so hungry that he was ready to beg for food, but he was too well dressed to be a beggar. He met a man selling old clothes and exchanged his European outfit for a Japanese-style coat, a faded hat and a few pieces of silver. He spent all the money he earned for breakfast at once.

A clown carrying a large sign printed in English attracted Passepartout's attention.

The sign announced that the circus would give one last performance that day before sailing to America. Passepartout followed the clown and arrived at the tent of the circus manager.

"Would you like a servant, sir?"

"No, I already have twoof them."

"Can I be of any use to you?"

"Not at all."

"That's too bad, for I would really like to go to America with you."

"Ah," said the manager, "you are not Japanese! Why are you dressed this way?"

"I am, in fact, a Frenchman."

"Can you make funny faces?"

"Of course."

"A French clown would be a huge success in America. Are you strong?"

"Yes," answered Passepartout, "especially after I eat a good meal."

"Can you sing?"

"Yes."

"If you can sing while standing on your head, with a top spinning on your left foot and a saber balanced on your right foot, then you're hired!"

Passepartout joined a group of clowns called the Long Noses. They wore winged costumes and had very long bamboo wood noses. They performed dancing tricks, and leapt about on each others noses. The last and most thrilling performance of the circus was to be a pyramid of clowns.

Passepartout and some of the other clowns had to form the bottom of the pyramid. They stood next to each other with their long noses pointing straight ahead. Another row of clowns balanced themselves on their noses, then another and so on. Each layer of the pyramid was narrower than the layer below. Finally, a single clown at the very top of the pyramid took his place, doing a splendid balancing act on the noses of the two clowns below him. The audience was ecstatic.

All of a sudden, Passepartout lost his balance and brought the clowns above him tumbling down.

The whole pyramid collapsed in a heap, as Passepartout ran off the stage. He had, visibly, spotted someone very familiar. Throwing himself at the feet of a man in the audience, he cried out. "My master, you're here!"

"Is that you?" exclaimed Phileas Fogg. "Let us hurry and catch the steamer!"

Fogg, Aouda and Passepartout left the circus tent quickly, after Mr. Fogg had paid the manager for the damage caused to the act by Passepartout, of course.

The party boarded the steamer at 16:30, just as it was about to depart. Passepartout was a funny sight, still wearing his long nose and his winged costume.

❑❑❑

Twenty Four

# Across the Pacific

Although Phileas Fogg and Aouda had missed the steamer Carnatic, they had reached Japan only one day after Passepartout did. As their small boat, the *Tankadere,* sailed into Shanghai, Captain John Bunsby signaled the steamer, which was just setting out for Japan. When the captain of the steamer spotted the *Tankadere's* flag flying at half-mast and heard the boom of the little cannon, the steamer's captain thought the little boat was in danger and steered over to help. Phileas Fogg paid John Bunsby his reward along with an extra 550 pounds before boarding the steamer with Aouda. They reached Japan on the morning of November 14.

Fogg learned that Passepartout had arrived on the Carnatic the day before. He hoped to find his servant before the American steamer departed that very night, but Yokohama was so huge that searching for him seemed futile.

Pure chance had brought Fogg to the circus. He would never have recognized Passepartout in his clown costume on stage. The servant, however, had spotted Fogg and, in his excitement, had lost his balance. As a result, the whole pyramid had come toppling down.

Passepartout decided not to tell his master about his conversation with Detective Fix back in Hong Kong. He simply explained that he had not shown up because he had drunk too much liquor and smoked too much opium. Phileas Fogg forgave him and handed him some money to buy real clothes. Within an hour, the clown costume and the long nose were cast off, and were nothing but a bad memory.

Phileas Fogg and his party sailed from Yokohama to San Francisco, California, on the steamer *General* Grant. Traveling at a steady 12 miles an hour, she could cross the Pacific Ocean in 21 days, thus arriving on December 2. This schedule would give Phileas Fogg time to reach New York by December 11 and London by December 20. He was not due back at the Reform Club until December 21.

Aouda worried that something else may

just obstruct their journey again and delay them. Passepartout, however, explained that they had already made it past the strange countries of China and Japan and that nothing could possibly go wrong in an advanced country like America.

Aouda was beginning to fall in love with Phileas Fogg. Besides being thankful to him for saving her life, she considered him to be praiseworthy and kind. Fogg, however, remained cold and quiet, and no one, could deduce his inner thoughts.

Nine days after leaving Yokohama, Phileas Fogg had traveled across exactly one half of the world. On November 23, the *General Grunt* was precisely 180 degrees across the globe from London. Fogg had used up more than half of the 80 days, however, because it wasn't possible to make the entire voyage in a straight line around the globe. Such a trip would have been about 12,000 miles. In fact, Fogg had already used up 52 days and traveled 17,500 miles in a journey totaling about 26,000 miles. Thus, he had completed more than two thirds of his trip and had 28 days left.

Best of all, Fix was no longer around to bother them, or so Mr. Fogg presumed.

On November 23, Passepartout noticed that his watch, which he had refused to reset according to Fix's advice, showed exactly the same time as the ship's clock. Passepartout was unaware of the fact that, considering they were halfway across the world from London, there was a 12 hour time difference.

Detective Fix was also aboard the *General Grant.* He had gone to the English consul in Yokohama and finally received the arrest warrant for Phileas Fogg. The warrant had been sent aboard the steamer Carnatic itself. However, since Fogg had already left English territory, the warrant would be no good until he returned to England. The detective was left with no alternative now: he would have to simply follow Mr. Fogg throughout the rest of his journey around the world.

"It seems like the rogue really does plan to go around the world to throw the police off his track," Fix said to himself. "The problem is that Fogg has spent so much money already that there might not be anything left for my reward when I finally arrest him."

Fix had recognized Passepartout, even in his clown costume, right when he and Aouda had boarded the *General Grant.* The detective wanted to remain out of sight, but that very day he ran into the servant on the deck. Passepartout grabbed him by the throat and knocked him sprawling on the floor.

"Can I have a word with you?" asked Fix, gasping.

"No, you may not."

"In your master's interests."

Passepartout unwillingly followed Fix.

"You knocked me down with your fists, and I deserved it," said the detective."Now, listen to me! Till now, I have been an enemy to Phileas Fogg, but now I'm prepared to assist him."

"So you finally believe that he's an honest man like I told you?"

"No, I still believe he's a scoundrel," answered Fix. "However, we will not know of his true intentions until we reach England. I have tried my best to force Fogg to remain on English soil, just so that I could arrest him. That is the sole reason why I sent the Bombay priests after you, got you drunk in Hong Kong, prevented you from meeting up with your master, and made Fogg miss the steamer to Yokohama."

Passepartout listened quietly but kept his fists clenched.

"Fogg seems to be returning to England," continued Fix. "I want to see him get there as quickly as possible. This is in your interest too."

"Very well," answered Passepartout, "but I'll break your neck if you do anything else to hinder or harm my master."

On December 3, the *General Grant* sailed into San Francisco harbor. Phileas Fogg had reached America exactly on schedule!

Twenty Five

# Colonel Proctor

A train was due to leave San Francisco for New York at 6:00 in the evening. Fogg and Aouda ate lunch and then went to the consulate for a visa. They ran into Detective Fix on the way.

"I had no idea we all traversed the Pacific on the same steamer," Fix lied, faking surprise again. "By the way, I have to return to England on business. I hope to have the pleasure of your company for the rest of the trip."

"My pleasure," answered Phileas Fogg, who still didn't have the faintest idea that Fix was a detective. The three of them walked toward Montgomery Street, where a huge crowd had assembled.

"Hurrah for Camerfield!" cried some voices. "Hurrah for Mandiboy!" cried others.

It was a political rally.

"We should leave," warned Fix. "Englishmen should keep away out of American politics."

Phileas Fogg, along with Fix, however, was already surrounded by the voters favoring Camerfield on one side, and by those favoring Mandiboy on the other. While Fogg struggled to shield Aouda, a tall, broad-shouldered man with a red beard and a flushed face raised his clenched fist. Fogg would have received a terrible blow had not Fix stepped in between him and his attacker. The blow crushed the detective's silk hat and knocked him to the ground.

"Yankee!" shouted Phileas Fogg to the American.

"Englishman!" screamed the ruffian. "We shall meet again. What's your name?"

"Phileas Fogg. What's yours?"

"Colonel Stamp Proctor."

Having finally escaped the mob, Fogg and Fix approached a tailor to have their rumpled clothes ironed. Then they met Passepartout for dinner. Aouda told him about their adventure, and Passepartout was pleased that Fix had indeed behaved like a friend rather than a troublemaker.

After dinner, Phileas Fogg and his party hired a carriage to take them to the railroad station. The train for New York was boarding.

"I must return to America someday to even the score with Colonel Proctor," said Fogg. "An Englishman has to defend his honor."

## Twenty Six

# An Encounter With The Buffaloes

San Francisco and New York are 3,768 miles apart. Back in 1872, the year this story has been set in, it took a train seven days to cover that distance. If Fogg reached New York by December 11, he could catch the trans-Atlantic steamer for Liverpool, England.

The first hindrance on the railroad was a herd of buffalo crossing the tracks. The herd numbered in thousands, and the buffalo moved very slowly. Phileas Fogg, as always, contended to wait. Passepartout, however, was enraged. He wanted to shoot the animals, but he knew that only a small number would actually die and that their bodies would completely block the track. There was nothing to do but wait patiently.

"What a country!" shouted Passepartout. "Animals should not be allowed to stop trains! Why not just run the buffalo down?"

In fact, the force of the engine against the buffalo could easily derail the train, thus causing an even worse delay.

It took three hours for all the buffalo to cross the tracks. The train could not move on until sundown. At 8:00, it reached Salt Lake City, Utah.

Twenty Seven

# Salt Lake City and the Mormons

Salt Lake City was the center of the Mormon religion. Mormon leaders often gave sermons aboard railroad trains, seeking more followers. Passepartout, who had heard that the Mormons were permitted to have more than one wife, decided to attend a sermon by a certain Elder Hitch.

Most of the audience quickly lost interest in the lecture, and soon Passepartout found himself alone in the car with the Mormon. Elder Hitch shouted, "We Mormons will never bow to force and pressure! We have been driven out of many parts of the United States, but we will continue to practice our religion! Will you join us, brother?"

"No!" snapped Passepartout, leaving Elder hitch dumbstruck, as the last member of his audience left too. Passepartout walked swiftly back to Phileas Fogg's car. The train's whistle was announcing that they were ready to leave the Mormon town and continue their journey east.

As the train was about to pull out of the Salt Lake City station, a man ran onto the platform, dashed along the track breathlessly and jumped aboard the moving train. When he caught his breath, he declared that he had run away after a quarrel with his wife.

"How many other wives do you have, anyway?' "asked Passepartout, amusedly.

"I have only one wife," the man replied, "and that is quite enough!"

❑❑❑

Twenty Eight

# Across the bridge

On December 7, the train stopped at the River station, and Aouda caught sight of Colonel Proctor on the platform.

Shocked to see him, she whispered to Passepartout, "We must keep this man away from Mr. Fogg!"

"Don't worry," said Fix. "Before he deals with Mr Fogg, he must confront me."

"Mr. Fogg will not let anyone else fight for him, Mr Fix. He said that he would definitely return to America to settle scores with the colonel. If they catch sight of each other now, something terrible might happen!"

"Listen!" said Passepartout. "Let's just ensure that Mr. Fogg doesn't leave the car until we reach New York. That way, he won't see Colonel Proctor. The best way to keep him in his car is to indulge him in a game of whist."

Passepartout produced two decks of cards.

All of a sudden, a loud whistle sounded, and the train came to a screeching halt. Fogg sent Passepartout to find out what was wrong. The engineer explained that the bridge at Medicine Bow, Wyoming, was not strong enough for the train to cross.

"We have wired Omaha, Nebraska, for a train," the engineer added, "but it won't reach Medicine Bow for at least six hours. It will take one that long to walk to Medicine Bow, anyhow."

"But Medicine Bow is only a mile from here," said Colonel Proctor.

"Yes," replied the engineer, "but it's across the river!"

"Can't we cross by boat?" asked Passepartout.

"That's impossible. The rains have flooded the river. We'd have to go ten miles to find a ford for crossing."

This would cause a major delay. In this case, Phileas Fogg's banknotes could do nothing about it! Fogg, however, was too busy playing whist to pay attention to what had happened.

"Gentlemen, there may be a way to cross the bridge after all," said the engineer.

"But the bridge is unsteady," said

Passepartout.

"It doesn't matter. If the train traverses it at top speed, we may have a chance to get across.' Passepartout thought it was too dangerous.

"It'll be safer to cross the bridge on foot, and then wait for the train to follow," he muttered, but no one was listening.

"Don't be scared!" said Colonel Proctor.

"All aboard!" shouted the conductor.

Phileas Fogg never even lifted his head from the card table.

The engineer backed up the train for almost a mile in order to get a good start. The train then lurched forward again, picking up speed until it reached 100 miles an hour.

Suddenly, in a flash, the train was over the bridge! It went five miles further on the other side before the engineer could bring it to a halt. The passengers were all safe, but the moment the train traversed the bridge, it fell with a loud crash into the river below.

Twenty Nine

# Colonel Proctor And The Indian Attack

Phileas Fogg's journey from San Francisco to New York was almost half over. The train had crossed 1,382 miles in three days. In another four days they would reach New York. Mr. Fogg was exactly on time.

Fogg and Detective Fix were playing whist so absorbedly that they didn't hear the man who had come up behind them.

"I would play a diamond, Englishman!" shouted Colonel Stamp Proctor.

Phileas Fogg laid the ten of spades on the table.

"I would rather have diamonds played than spades," the colonel insisted, moving toward Fogg, with an action to grab the card. "You really don't know how to play whist."

Suddenly, Detective Fix rose to his feet.

"You forget, Colonel Proctor, that you must deal with me first, for you struck and insulted me in San Francisco."

"No, Mr. Fix," said Phileas Fogg. "This is my affair and I'll handle it. The colonel has insisted that I play a spade. He won't get away with it!"

"I'm ready to fight a duel with you," said Colonel Proctor. "You choose the weapon."

Phileas Fogg went out to the platform, followed by the American.

"Sir, I am in a great hurry to return to Europe," Fogg explained. "I cannot allow anything to delay me. Will you meet me here in six months?"

"You're just looking for a way out of this. You do not wish to play against me. It's now or never!"

said Colonel Proctor.

"Are you going to New York?", demanded Mr Fogg.

"No. I'm going to Plum Creek," said Proctor. "That's the next station. The train will stop there for ten minutes. That will give us time to exchange a few shots."

"Very well," said Fogg. "We'll stop at Plum Creek."

He returned to his car to finish the game of whist.

When the train reached Plum Creek station, the conductor shouted, "Gentlemen, you can't get off! We're 20 minutes late and can't stop here!"

"But we must fight a duel!" cried Fogg.

"How about fighting as the train moves along?", suggested the conductor, and the two men agreed. The last car of the train was chosen for the duel. Phileas Fogg and Colonel Proctor were to march, toward each other from opposite ends of the car and then fire their revolvers. As the countdown began, gunfire was heard from the front end of the train. A band of Sioux Indians had attacked! They ran through the cars, fighting hand to hand with the screaming passengers. Then they climbed into the engine and tried to stop the train. Instead of closing the steam valve, however, they opened it wide, causing the train to rush forward at top speed.

"Unless the train is stopped in five minutes, we'll all be lost!" shouted the conductor: "Fort Kearney is only two miles away, and the soldiers there can help us!"

"The train will be stopped!" said Passepartout. Before Phileas Fogg could stop him, he opened a door and slipped under the car. A few minutes later, the train came to a stop a few feet from Kearney station.

Thirty

# Rescuing Passepartout

By holding onto the metal chains under the cars, Passepartout had managed to swing from the back end of the train to the front. He had loosened the safety chain that connected the engine to the other cars, and the jolts of the rapidly moving train broke the engine loose. When the train came to a stop by Fort Kearney, however, Passepartout and two other passengers were missing.

The Indians, who had fled at the first sight of the soldiers, had taken the three as prisoners.

"I will find Passepartout, dead or alive!" declared Phileas Fogg to Aouda.

This decision might well cost Fogg his 20,000-pound bet. He could not afford to lose a single day, but he could not abandon his faithful servant.

"Three passengers have been taken prisoner," said Fogg to the commander at Fort

Kearney. "Will you go after the Sioux?"

"I can't do that, sir. I must protect the fort from Indian attacks."

"The lives of three men are at stake," Fogg insisted.

"That may be true, but I cannot risk the lives of a 100 men to save three."

"Very well, then, I will go alone!"

"You can't handle the Indians alone!"

"Do you expect me to let Passepartout die after he saved all of our lives?" asked Fogg.

"You are a brave man. I will send 30 men to assist you," said the commander, impressed by Fogg's daring. Fogg promised to divide 5,000 dollars among them if they helped him bring the prisoners back alive.

Aouda and Fix waited anxiously for Fogg to return. Fix feared that the "robber" might escape for good with the stolen money.

Suddenly a whistle sounded. The engineer was running the locomotive back to join the stranded train.

"We must start at once," said the conductor. "We're way behind schedule!"

"What about the prisoners?" Aouda asked.

"We cannot wait for them!"

"Then I will stay behind," she said.

The train sped off into the distance. Night

came, and there was still no sign of Fogg and the soldiers. At dawn, the fort commander was ready to give up on those thirty soldiers and declare them lost. Suddenly, in the distance appeared the large troop of soldiers, accompanied by Fogg and the prisoners.

❐❐❐

Thirty One

# Sledges And All!

"Where is the train?" asked Phileas Fogg, as he reached Aouda.

"Gone," said Aouda, sobbing with relief in Passepartout's arms.

"When will the next train pass through?"

"Not until this evening."

Fogg was already 20 hours behind schedule, and he had to reach New York by 9:00 in the evening on December 11 in order to catch the steamer for Liverpool.

"If you are really, in such a great hurry, perhaps I can help you regain some time," offered Fix, who, at Fogg's request, had stayed to take care of Aouda at Kearney station.

"What do you have in mind, Mr. Fix?"

"There is an American named Mudge who has a sledge here-a sledge with sails! He can drive us to Omaha. It will be easy to catch a train to New York from there."

The sledge was designed to carry passengers from one station to another when heavy snow blocked the train tracks. The strong winds on the prairie could carry a sledge at a speed as fast as that of an express train. At 5:00, the sledge was ready to start off. The passengers wrapped themselves in warm traveling cloaks. The two great sails were hoisted, and the wind pushed the vehicle over the snow-covered prairie at a speed of 40 miles an hour. The distance from Fort Kearney to Omaha was about 200 miles. With luck, it could be covered in five hours.

Mudge had a personal interest in reaching Omaha on time, because Phileas Fogg had promised him a generous reward.

The sledge was aided by strong winds, which, nevertheless, left the passengers chilled. Howling bands of prairie wolves nipped at the back of the vehicle, and Passepartout kept his gun ready to shoot them if necessary.

They finally reached Omaha at noon. Fogg paid him and went directly to the railroad station. A train took Fogg's party to Chicago, where another train was waiting to make the

900 mile trip to New York.

At 11:45 P.M. on December 11, Fogg, Passepartout, Aouda and Fix arrived at New York harbor. But alas! The steamer they were to take to Liverpool, the *China*, had already set sail.

❑❑❑

Thirty Two

# Captain Speedy and the *Henrietta*

*The China* had been Phileas Fogg's last hope of winning his bet. But 'he remained as calm as ever. The travelers hired a carriage to take them to the St. Nicholas Hotel on Broadway. Phileas Fogg spent a restful night, but the others were too upset to sleep.

The next day was December 12, with nine days to go before Fogg's scheduled return to the Reform Club on December 21. The gentleman's entire fortune was at stake, with his last chance of ever making it back to England on time seeming bleak.

After ordering Aouda and Passepartout to be ready to leave New York at a moment's notice, Mr. Fogg left the hotel and went to the harbor. When he found a ship prepared to set sail, he climbed aboard.

"I am Phileas Fogg, of London," he greeted the captain.

"And my name is Andrew Speedy, the captain of the *Henrietta.*"

"Are you going out to sea?"

"Yes, in an hour."

"Does your ship travel fast?"

"Her speed is 11 or 12 knots."

"That's very good! Will you take me and a few other people to Liverpool?"

"No, I'm going to Bordeaux, in France. Besides, I never carry passengers. They get in my way."

"How much money will help to persuade you?" asked Fogg, using his typical way to entice people into helping him out.

"Money means nothing to me," replied the captain firmly.

"If you won't take me along, let me buy the *Henrietta* from you."

"No."

"Will you take me to Bordeaux, then?"

"No, not even if you pay me $200."

"I will pay you $2,000!"

"Each of the four crew members?"

"Yes, each one."

"All right," said Captain Speedy."I will sail promptly at 9:00."

"We'll be ready," Fogg replied.

It was already 8:30. Phileas Fogg gathered

up Aouda, Passepartout and Fix and brought them to the *Henrietta.* When Fix learnt of the money Fogg would be paying the crew of the *Henrietta,* he was dejected. Mr Fogg would have no money left by the time they were safely back in England. When he would be arrested, there would be barely any money left to return to the bank.

Thirty Three

# Phileas Fogg Takes Charge

By the time the *Henrietta* sailed into the Atlantic Ocean, Phileas Fogg was in charge. He had bribed the crew to lock Captain Speedy in his cabin and then veer the ship to Liverpool instead of Bordeaux.

America and England lay 3,000 miles apart. If the weather was calm throughout, the journey could easily be made by December 21. The engineer, however, informed "Captain" Fogg that there wasn't enough fuel to reach England.

"Feed all the fires until the coal is gone!", Fogg ordered.

Within minutes, the *Hen*rietta's smokestacks sent up great clouds of steam. On December 18, however, it became clear that the coal would be gone by nightfall.

"Bring Captain Speedy to the deck" commanded Phileas Fogg.

"Where are we?" bellowed the captain.

"We are 707 miles from Liverpool," Fogg replied very calmly.

"You are indeed a pirate!"

"I have sent for you, sir, to ask you to sell me your ship."

"No! Never!"

'But I shall have to burn her-at least her upper part. The coal has run out."

"Burn my ship? The *Henrietta is* worth 50,000 dollars!"

"Here is 60,000 dollars," said Fogg. "You see, if I don't reach London by 8:45 P.M. on December 21, I shall lose 20,000 pounds. I missed the steamer at New York, and you refused to take me to Liverpool."

"I made a wise decision, anyhow," replied the captain, "for you have paid me handsomely for my ship!"

Phileas Fogg ordered all the wooden parts of the *Henrietta* burned. The crew tore the ship down to its flat metal hull.

On December 20, with the fires still burning, Fogg sighted the coast of Ireland. By evening, however, the steam pressure, which had been kept up by the burning wood, was about to give out completely. Mr. Fogg had less than 24 hours to reach London.

"We shall dock at Queenstown," he announced.

The transatlantic steamers brought all the mail to this Irish port. The mail was then carried to the Irish capital, Dublin, by express train and then the fastest available boats transported the mail to Liverpool. Phileas Fogg decided to take the same route as the mail, in order to gain 12 hours over the Atlantic steamers in getting to London.

At 1:00 in the morning, the *Henrietta* docked at Queenstown. Fogg, Aouda, Passepartout and Detective Fix boarded the express train at once. It left the station at 1:30 and arrived in Dublin at daybreak. The travelers then caught a steamer, and on December 21 at 11:40, they sailed into Liverpool. Phileas Fogg was now only six hours away from London by train.

Instinctively, Fix proudly walked up to Mr. Fogg, and declared, "I now arrest you in the name of the Queen of England."

Thirty Four

# Phileas Fogg is Detained

Passepartout leapt at Fix but some policemen appeared from behind him and held him back. He took his revolver out, and just managed to escape being shot himself.

Fogg was now behind bars.

"Why didn't I tell my master what Fix was really up to?" Passepartout cried, holding himself responsible for what had happened. He had cost Phileas Fogg 20,000 pounds.

Fogg, surprisingly, sat relaxedly in his prison cell, displaying no emotion whatsoever. He still had almost nine hours to reach London, and the journey took only six. He laid his watch on the table and watched its hands move ever closer to the fateful hour of 8:45.

He thought of escaping wuite a few times, but soon altogether gave up the idea. The door was locked and the window heavily barred. After walking around the room, he sat down and took his diary out of his pocket.

On the page for December 21, he wrote, "Liverpool, 80th day, 11:40 A.M."

The clock in the jailhouse struck 1:00. Fogg noticed that his watch was two hours slow.

At exactly 2:33, Passepartout, Aouda and Detective Fix rushed into the room. Fix was breathless, and his clothes and hair were disheveled.

"Sir," he stammered, "sir, please forgive me! The bank robber was arrested three days ago! You simply resembled him a lot. Now you are free to go!"

Phileas Fogg walked up to Fix and, with an unexpected, yet powerful blow of his arms, knocked him flat to the floor. Fogg, Aouda and Passepartout then hastily left the jailhouse, called a taxi, and sped towards the railroad station.

It was 2:40. The express train for London had already left 35 minutes ago. Phileas Fogg ordered a special train, but it would not be ready until 3:00. Mr. Fogg, as always, offered the engineer a generous reward for getting him to London as fast as possible, boarded the train with Aouda and his faithful servant.

If the tracks had been clear, they could have made the trip in five and a half hours. There were quite a few delays, however, and it was already 8:50 when the train reached London.

Phileas Fogg was five minutes too late. Those five minutes had cost him everything. All was lost.

Thirty Five

# Aouda's Proposal

Phileas Fogg still took his loss very bravely. He was, still, however, baffled by the idea that after braving several dangers throughout his voyage, he had been falsely detained by an unexpected detective, who had been on his trail all along- the most unexpected of obstructions. All that remained of the thick roll of banknotes he had set out with were a few pounds. The rest of his fortune, amounting to 20,000 pounds was at the bank, ready to be transferred to the gentlemen at the Reform Club. Fogg's trip cost so much money that even winning the bet would not have made him rich.

Aouda was given a room to stay in Mr. Fogg's large house. Passepartout returned to his room and immediately went on to switch his gas off, which had already been burning for 80 whole days. The bill from the gas company awaited him in his mailbox. Phileas

Fogg went to bed at midnight as usual, but one could be unsure of whether he slept at all, with such a huge loss impending. The next day, amazingly, he did not get up to leave home for the Reform Club at 11:30. In fact he spent the entire day alone in his room. Finally, at 7:30, he went downstairs to talk with Aouda.

"Please forgive me for bringing you all the way to England," he began. "When I took you away from India, I was a wealthy man, and I had thought that I would readily have given away a large sum of money to you, to keep you happy and independent. But, as of now, I am ruined! Completely ruined!"

"It is I who should beg forgiveness, Mr. Fogg. If you had not stopped to lend me a hand and save me from the clutches of death, you would have gained on a lot of time right then."

"But madam! You would have have certainly been put to death if you had stayed in India! I had to bring you over to a. safe place. I still hope to put what little money I have left at your disposal."

"But what will become of you, sir?"

"I don't need anything, madam."

"Maybe your friends could help you out."

"I have no friends."

"Your relatives?"

"I no longer have any relatives."

"That really is a pity, for you have no one to confide your sorrows to."

Aouda instinctively took Phileas Fogg's hand in hers.

"Do you desire both a friend and a relative? Will you have me as your wife?"

Phileas Fogg's lips trembled, and his eyes were bright.

"I love you," he said, unexpectedly.

Fogg immediately asked Passepartout to contact the Reverend Samuel Wilson.

"When do you wish to get married, sir?"

"Tomorrow, Monday," replied his master.

Passepartout hurried to the Reverend's house. It was already past 8:00.

Thirty Six

# At The Reform Club

On december 17, when Mr Fogg was on the verge of completing his around-the-world-trip, the real bank robber, a Mr. James Strand, had already been arrested. All at once, Fogg, who had once been sought by the London police, was restored to the title of a gentleman.

A large crowd had already collected outside the Reform Club on Saturday evening, December 21. As the fateful hour of 8:45 neared, the people's enthusiasm increased.

At 8:20, the gentlemen with whom Fogg had made the wager assembled in the saloon, right where the bet had been laid.

"What time did the last train arrive from Liverpool?" asked Thomas Flanagan.

"At 7:23," replied Gautier Ralph. "The next train doesn't come until 12:10."

"If he came by the 7:23 train, he would have been here by now," said Andrew Stuart:

"Let's also remember," said John Sullivan, "that Mr. Fogg has not sent us a single message since he left, even though there are telegraph lines in all the places he visited. He is surely mislaid somewhere."

"There's no doubt about that," said Stuart. "The *China*, the only steamer Fogg could have possibly taken from New York to arrive here right on time, arrived yesterday. I enwuired about him myself, but his name wasn't on the passenger list."

"All that is left, then, is to present Phileas Fogg's check at the bank tomorrow," Ralph concluded heartily.

At exactly 8:44, a roar went up from the crowd outside the Reform Club. The gentlemen in the saloon stopped playing whist and stood up nervously from the table. A moment later, Phileas Fogg entered the room.

"Here I am, gentlemen!" he said, a big smile splitting his face.

❐❐❐

Thirty Seven

# Fogg Wins After All

Phileas Fogg did win his bet after all!

He had always made frequent note of the time but had, at the same time, also forgotten that by traveling eastward, or toward the sun, he was able to gain a whole day at the end of his trip around the world.

It was Passepartout who broke the good news. He returned from Reverend Wilson's house shouting, "Master, it's impossible for you to get married tomorrow!"

"Tomorrow is Sunday! We have arrived home 24 hours ahead of time! It is Saturday today master, but you have only five minutes to make it to the reform club, sir. It is 8:40 already."

Phileas Fogg entered the club with only seconds to spare. He thus won 20,000 pounds, having, however, spent almost 19,000 on his journey. His honor meant much more to him than money, however.

He divided the remaining 1,000 pounds between Passepartout and Fix, whom he had forgiven. The servant had to pay the gas bill out of his own share.

Having settled with the gentlemen of the Reform Club, Fogg hurried home to Aouda. "Do you still wish to marry me?" he asked.

"I should ask you that question," she replied. "When you agreed to the wedding, you thought you were ruined. Now you are a wealthy man once again."

"Pardon me, madam, but my fortune belongs to you. If you had not proposed a wedding, Passepartout would not have gone to the Reverend Wilson's house, and I would have been unaware of my mistake and never have made it to the Reform Club on time."

Phileas Fogg and Aouda were married the following day. Passepartout, who had rescued the bride in the first place became the best man.

At daybreak the following morning, Passepartout awoke with a pang of excitement. He rushed to his master's door, and knocked on it gleefully.

Mr. Fogg opened the door sleepily, and gave a huge yawn.

"What is it, Passepartout?"

"Master, I have just realized that we could have easily made our around-the-world trip in a total of simply 78 days."

"Yes, but only if we hadn't stopped to rescue Aouda. It was worth traveling for one extra day."

"Yes, master," said Passepartout, and then left to attend to his daily chores, chortling to himself.